# PRINCE HARRY

Tammy
Gagne

**Mitchell Lane**
PUBLISHERS
2001 SW 31st Avenue
Hallandale, FL 33009
www.mitchelllane.com

**Mitchell Lane**
PUBLISHERS

Printing    1    2    3    4    5    6    7    8    9

### A Robbie Reader Biography

Aaron Rodgers
Abigail Breslin
Adam Levine
Adrian Peterson
Albert Einstein
Albert Pujols
Aly and AJ
Andrew Luck
AnnaSophia Robb
Ariana Grande
Ashley Tisdale
Brenda Song
Brittany Murphy
Bruno Mars
Buster Posey
Carmelo Anthony
Charles Schulz
Chris Johnson
Clayton Kershaw
Cliff Lee
Colin Kaepernick
Dak Prescott
Dale Earnhardt Jr.
Darius Rucker
David Archuleta
Debby Ryan
Demi Lovato

Derek Carr
Derrick Rose
Donovan McNabb
Drake Bell & Josh Peck
Dr. Seuss
Dustin Pedroia
Dwayne Johnson
Dwyane Wade
Dylan & Cole Sprouse
Ed Sheeran
Emily Osment
Ezekiel Elliott
Hailee Steinfeld
Harry Styles
Hilary Duff
Jamie Lynn Spears
Jennette McCurdy
Jeremy Lin
Jesse McCartney
Jimmie Johnson
Joe Flacco
Johnny Gruelle
Jonas Brothers
Keke Palmer
Kristaps Porzingis
Larry Fitzgerald

LeBron James
Meghan Markle
Mia Hamm
Michael Strahan
Miguel Cabrera
Miley Cyrus
Miranda Cosgrove
Philo Farnsworth
Prince Harry
Raven-Symoné
Rixton
Robert Griffin III
Roy Halladay
Shaquille O'Neal
Story of Harley-Davidson
Sue Bird
Syd Hoff
Tiki Barber
Tim Howard
Tim Lincecum
Tom Brady
Tony Hawk
Troy Polamalu
Tyler Perry
Victor Cruz
Victoria Justice

**Library of Congress Cataloging-in-Publication Data**
Names: Gagne, Tammy, author.
Title: Prince Harry / by Tammy Gagne.
Description: Hallandale, FL : Mitchell Lane Publishers, 2019. | Series: A Robbie reader | Includes bibliographical references and index. | Audience: Ages 5-9.
Identifiers: LCCN 2018008728 | ISBN 9781680202922 (library bound)
Subjects: LCSH: Henry, Prince, grandson of Elizabeth II, Queen of Great Britain, 1984- —Juvenile literature. | Princes—Great Britain—Biography—Juvenile literature.
Classification: LCC DA591.A45 G35 2018 | DDC 941.086092 [B] —dc23
LC record available at https://lccn.loc.gov/2018008728

eBook ISBN: 978-1-68020-293-9

**ABOUT THE AUTHOR:** Tammy Gagne is the author of numerous books for adults and children, including *Meghan Markle* and *Ed Sheeran* for Mitchell Lane Publishers. She resides in northern New England with her husband and son. One of her favorite pastimes is visiting schools to speak to kids about the writing process.

**PUBLISHER'S NOTE:** The following story has been thoroughly researched and to the best of our knowledge represents a true story. While every possible effort has been made to ensure accuracy, the publisher will not assume liability for damages caused by inaccuracies in the data, and makes no warranty on the accuracy of the information contained herein. This story has not been authorized or endorsed by Prince Harry.

# CONTENTS

Words in bold type can be found in the glossary.

Prince Harry grew up in the center of the public eye. Although he went through some difficult years, he is now a mature and capable young man with a purpose. He wants to continue the legacy begun by his mother, Diana Princess of Wales, by dedicating his life to helping others.

# 1 TALKING ABOUT IT

"**M**om, I need to talk to you." Grace's straightforward tone made it clear that whatever was on her mind was important.

"What's up, love?" her mother asked as she closed her laptop, ready to listen.

"I have a mental illness," Grace said.

"Yes," her mother replied. "Did you have a bad day? Did you forget to take your medication?" Grace's father had passed away the previous year after battling cancer. A few months later, she was **diagnosed** with a condition called depression. Losing a family member is never easy, but for Grace the feelings of sadness had gotten worse instead of better.

> Grace's father had passed away the previous year after battling cancer.

"No, it was actually a pretty good day. I got a B+ on my algebra test, and my friend Mackenzie invited me to the movies this weekend." She then added, "And I took my meds this morning."

> Prince Harry is no stranger to grief. When he was just 12, his mother, Diana, Princess of Wales, was killed in a car accident.

"So what did you want to talk about?" her mother asked.

"I just wanted to practice saying it out loud. I was watching a YouTube video of Prince Harry and his family about the importance of talking about mental illness. They said it is part of the healing process. Harry said it can be easier to talk about a physical injury, because everyone can see something like that. But mental illness affects people just as much."

"He's a pretty smart guy," her mother said with a smile. "I hope you know that you can talk to me about anything on good days or bad ones."

"Oh, I know," Grace assured her. "Would you like to see the video?" she asked.

"I would," her mother said as she reopened her computer. "Maybe we can share it on my Facebook page. It sounds like something that other people might benefit from watching, too."

Prince Harry is no stranger to **grief**. When he was just 12, his mother, Diana, Princess of Wales, was killed in a car accident. It was a devastating loss for Harry

*Prince Harry was among the many mourners who left flowers and other mementos at London's Kensington Palace to honor his mother following her tragic death. This part of the palace grounds has since been transformed into the White Garden, which is dedicated to Diana's memory.*

and his older brother, Prince William, who was 15. Now adults, they both want to help other people facing their own struggles with mental health. With the help of William's wife, Catherine, the princes formed Heads Together. One of the biggest goals of the campaign is reducing the **stigma** of mental illness so more people can get the help they need.

*Duke and Duchess of Cambridge, Prince William and Catherine, and Prince Harry attend a training day for the Heads Together team for the London Marathon at Olympic Park on February 5, 2017, in London, England.*

# 2 THE YOUNGER PRINCE

On September 15, 1984, the Prince and Princess of Wales welcomed their second child at St. Mary's Hospital in West London. Charles and Diana named their new son Henry Charles Albert David. But they–and the rest of the world–would call him "Harry." Prince Harry was an active, outgoing young boy who always seemed to be smiling. This earned him another nickname, the "Happy Prince." At home the mischievous young prince had a third nickname. His mother is said to have called him "Your Royal Naughtiness."

> **Prince Harry was an active, outgoing young boy who always seemed to be smiling.**

When he was old enough to go to school, Harry entered Mrs. Mynors' Nursery School. It was the same school his brother William had attended. Even though the young princes were part of the British Royal Family, their mother wanted them to have as many normal childhood experiences as possible. She regularly took them to places other kids went such as amusement parks and movie theaters. She even took them to fast food restaurants occasionally.

**Growing up the younger brother of Prince William, Harry was third in line to the British throne. Their father was first, William second.**

In 1989, Harry joined William at Wetherby Pre-Prep in London. Three years later, Harry entered the Ludgrove Preparatory School, a boarding school for boys ages eight to 13. By this time he had already earned a reputation as a capable athlete. He especially enjoyed horseback riding and playing **polo**.

*Princess Diana and Prince Harry during the 50th anniversary of VE (Victory in Europe) Day on May 7, 1995*

Many younger brothers often get compared to their older siblings. But in Harry's case the comparisons were a mighty public affair. Growing up the younger brother of Prince William, Harry was third in line to the British throne. Their father was first, William second. After Harry was born, some people even referred to the young boys

*Harry proved to be a talented polo player soon after he started playing the sport.*

as "the heir and the spare." This meant that if for any reason William could not serve as king one day, Harry was there to take the job.

Harry spent a great deal of his younger years in his older brother's shadow. The British people often focus more attention on William, since he is more likely to become the king. At the same time, the British Royal Family expected Harry to serve the people in other ways. Although many people saw Harry as second to William, his position as the second son of Prince Charles gave Harry a certain amount of freedom, which he clearly enjoyed.

# 3 GREAT LOSSES

Being part of a royal family comes with a lot of pressure. Almost nothing happens to Harry or the rest of his family without the entire world knowing about it. The pressure is even greater when they go through rough times. The same year Harry entered Ludgrove, his parents decided to separate. Rumors about their troubled marriage put the family on the covers of **tabloids** for the next several years.

In 1996, Charles and Diana decided to get a divorce. Harry has said that he and William felt like they didn't get enough time with either parent after the split. "I don't pretend that we're the only people

In 1996, Charles and Diana decided to get a divorce.

to have to deal with that," he said in the documentary *Diana, Our Mother: Her Life and Legacy*, "but it was an interesting way to grow up."

> However, on September 6, the time came for Harry and his brother to join the public in saying goodbye to their beloved mother at her funeral.

When Diana died on August 31, 1997, the entire world mourned her death. But to Harry and William, the loss was even more devastating. The young brothers were on vacation with their father at Balmoral Castle in Scotland when the tragic car accident happened in France. **Paparazzi** were chasing the princess for photos when her car crashed in a Paris tunnel. In the days and weeks that followed, Queen Elizabeth II protected her grandsons from the extensive media coverage. She even hid newspapers so they wouldn't see them.

*Prince William (left), Prince Harry, and their father, Prince Charles, bow their heads as Princess Diana's coffin is taken out of Westminster Abbey following her funeral service.*

However, on September 6, the time came for Harry and his brother to join the public in saying goodbye to their beloved mother at her funeral. The boys had to walk behind her coffin in the funeral procession. In 2017, Harry told *Newsweek* that it was something no child should have to do. "Years after, I spent a long time in my life with my head buried in the sand, thinking, I don't want to be Prince Harry. I don't want this responsibility. I don't want this role."

In time he realized that serving as prince offered him the opportunity to carry on his mother's charitable legacy. Diana dedicated her life to many worthy causes. In 1995, she told the BBC that nothing gave her greater happiness than helping the most **vulnerable** members of society. Carrying on that work, Harry now tries to fill the need her passing left behind.

*Harry is pictured here in 2004 with a new friend, a four-year-old boy named Matsu Potsane. The two met while Harry volunteered some time at the Mant'ase Children's Home in Lesotho, South Africa.*

# 4 ACTING OUT AND GROWING UP

Harry's mischievous spirit reemerged during his adolescent years. The younger prince spent a fair amount of time living it up at parties while he attended Eton College. Occasionally, he got himself into trouble by drinking too much or making foolish choices. One such time was when he wore a Nazi costume, which included a **swastika**–a hateful symbol of Nazi Germany–to a party. Shortly after the event, Harry issued a public apology to everyone he offended with his actions. He certainly wasn't the first young person to make an inappropriate decision. But as a member of the royal family, people

> The younger prince spent a fair amount of time living it up at parties while he attended Eton College.

expected more of him. Fortunately, as Harry matured, he began making better decisions.

**Harry's army service lasted for 10 years and included two tours in Afghanistan. During this time he rose to the rank of captain.**

In 2006, Harry did something that his older brother could not do. He served on the front lines in Afghanistan after joining the Blues and Royals. Security concerns would have made it impossible for William to take on such a dangerous job. To lessen the risk Harry and his fellow soldiers faced, his whereabouts were kept secret for some time. If the public knew where he was, he likely would have become a target for the Taliban.

Harry's army service lasted for 10 years and included two tours in Afghanistan. During this time he rose to the rank of captain. He also became a skilled helicopter pilot. He spent much of his time as an Apache copilot and gunner. His experience in

*Prince Harry is seen here on patrol in the deserted town of Garmisir in Afghanistan. For most of the time he was stationed in the country, his whereabouts were kept a secret. Otherwise, he would have been a high-level target of the Taliban.*

*Prince Harry was known as Captain Wales when he was in the British Army. He is seen here in the cockpit of an Apache helicopter. He was a pilot/gunner from September of 2012 to January of 2013.*

the military inspired him to work with injured military veterans through charities such as Walking With The Wounded. In 2011, he spent four days on a trek to the North Pole with four wounded soldiers, an expedition that raised money for the charity. In 2013, he joined the charity's expedition to the South Pole. He is also actively involved in the Invictus Games. He created this international sporting event for wounded veterans.

*Harry had to take part in lots of training before beginning his trek to the North Pole with his Walking With The Wounded team in 2011.*

# 5 GETTING SERIOUS ABOUT THE FUTURE

For many years Harry was considered Great Britain's most eligible bachelor. When William married his longtime girlfriend, Catherine Middleton, in 2011, the media's focus on Harry's love life intensified. Many people wondered who would win the younger prince's heart. Although he dated many young women, Harry never seemed to be serious about any of them—until Meghan Markle came along.

Harry met the American actress in 2016 when a mutual friend introduced them in London. When they were seen together at

> Although he dated many young women, Harry never seemed to be serious about any of them—until Meghan Markle came along.

*Prince Harry and his new fiancée, Meghan Markle, shared their engagement with the public on November 27, 2017. They made the official announcement at the Sunken Gardens at Kensington Palace.*

various events in the months that followed, the media began printing stories about their suspected relationship. But Harry and Meghan were rather tight-lipped about whether they were romantically involved. They wanted to enjoy their **courtship** privately. After dating for a little over a year, the couple announced their engagement. They were married in May of 2018 in a highly celebrated royal wedding ceremony.

> Although no one knows when the couple will start a family, many people think Prince Harry would make a wonderful father.

Although no one knows when or if the couple will start a family, many people think Prince Harry would make a wonderful father. He is already the godparent of several friends' children. Harry has said that he thinks the key to being a good godparent is being a grown-up while still remaining somewhat childlike. He has also shared that he can play video games with the best of them.

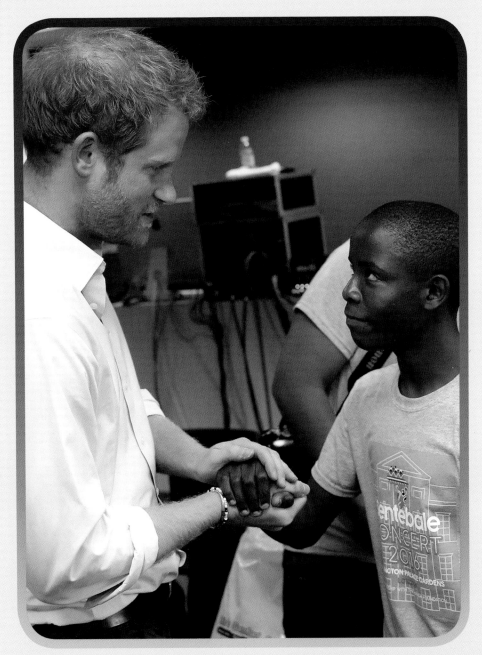

*Harry kept in touch with his friend Mutsu Potsane long after they first met in 2004. They are seen here when the 16-year-old was getting ready to sing as part of the Basotho Youth Choir at London's Brit School on June 27, 2016.*

Harry is also an enthusiastic uncle to William's young kids. The births of Prince William and Duchess Catherine's children have placed Harry sixth in line for the British throne today. But in 2017, he told the *Daily Mail* that he could never wish them away; he thinks his brother's kids are "the most amazing things ever." He has also said that Catherine is like the sister he never had.

*The royal family left to right: Duchess Camilla, Prince Charles, Prince George, Prince William, Catherine, Queen Elizabeth II, Prince Harry, and Prince Philip look out on the balcony of Buckingham Palace during the Trooping the Colour on June 13, 2015, in London, England.*

*Meghan Markle and Prince Harry, patron of the Invictus Games Foundation, attend the UK Team Trials for the Invictus Games Sydney 2018 at the University of Bath Sports Training Village on April 6, 2018, in Bath, England. The Invictus Games Sydney 2018 will take place from October 20-27 and will see over 500 competitors from 18 nations compete in 11 adaptive sports.*

While he is now even less likely to become the king, Harry's position in the royal family remains an important one. He often makes appearances on behalf of Queen Elizabeth. Prince Harry is deeply admired for both his military service and his charity work, and he plans to keep working with worthy causes in the future.

# CHRONOLOGY

**1984** Henry Charles Albert David, Prince of Wales, is born on September 15.

**2002** Prince Harry enters Ludgrove Preparatory School.

**1992** The Prince and Princess of Wales separate.

**1996** Prince Charles and Diana, Princess of Wales, divorce.

**1997** Diana is killed in a car accident in Paris.

**2003** He graduates from Eton College.

**2006** Prince Harry joins the Blues and Royals.

**2011** The prince joins injured soldiers on the Walking With The Wounded trek to the North Pole.

**2013** Harry joins another Walking With The Wounded trek, this time to the South Pole.

**2017** Prince Charles announces the engagement of his son, Prince Harry, to Ms. Meghan Markle.

**2018** Prince Harry weds Meghan Markle on May 19.

# FIND OUT MORE

Prince Harry. Official website of the British Royal Family.
https://www.royal.uk/prince-harry

# WORKS CONSULTED

Bulman, May. "Diana's humanitarian and charity legacy: from
landmines to leprosy." *The Independent*, August 31, 2017.
http://www.independent.co.uk/news/uk/home-news/
dianas-humanitarian-and-charity-legacy-from-landmines-
to-leprosy-a7911661.html

Campbell, Sarah. "Royal baby: 'The heir and the spare.'" BBC,
April 23, 2015. http://www.bbc.com/news/uk-29111548

"Charles and Diana divorce." The History Channel. http://www.
history.com/this-day-in-history/charles-and-diana-divorce

Durand, Carolyn. "Prince William, Prince Harry open up about
how they learned of their mother's death." ABC News,
August 23, 2017. http://abcnews.go.com/Entertainment/
prince-william-prince-harry-open-learned-mothers-death/
story?id=49362641

Gonzales, Erica. "Prince Harry and Kate Middleton Have the
Cutest Brother-Sister Relationship." *Harper's Bazaar*, June 22,
2017. http://www.harpersbazaar.com/celebrity/latest/
a10207370/prince-harry-kate-middleton-sibling-
relationship/

Lloyd, Robert. "Review: 'Diana, Our Mother: Her Life and
Legacy' offers no digging or analysis, but is moving all the
same." *Los Angeles Times*, July 23, 2017. http://www.latimes.
com/entertainment/tv/la-et-st-diana-our-mother-review-
20170724-story.html

Nguyen, Vi-An. "10 Wacky Facts About Prince Harry (Like His
Childhood Nickname!)." *Parade*, September 15, 2014.
https://parade.com/339064/viannguyen/happy-30th-
birthday-prince-harry-10-wacky-facts-about-the-royal-like-
his-childhood-nickname/

# WORKS CONSULTED

Nicol, Mark. "Harry is grounded: Prince to stay in army . . . but he will never fly combat helicopters again." DailyMail.com, February 21, 2015. http://www.dailymail.co.uk/news/article-2963393/Harry-grounded-Prince-stay-Army-never-fly-combat-helicopters-again.html

Perry, Simon. "Why Prince George Could Go to Boarding School as Young as Age 8." *People*, January 13, 2016. http://people.com/royals/why-prince-george-could-go-to-boarding-school-as-young-as-age-8/

"Prince Harry." Hello! https://us.hellomagazine.com/profiles/prince-harry/

"Prince Harry." Official website of the British Royal Family. https://www.royal.uk/prince-harry

"Prince Harry back from Walking With The Wounded trek." BBC, April 10, 2011. http://www.bbc.com/news/uk-13028941

"Prince Harry and team arrive at South Pole." BBC, December 13, 2013. http://www.bbc.com/news/uk-25354839

"Prince Harry's Military Career." Official website of the British Royal Family. https://www.royal.uk/prince-harrys-military-career

Proudfoot, Jenny. "Prince Harry just said the loveliest thing about Princess Charlotte and Prince George." *Marie Claire*, June 28, 2017. http://www.marieclaire.co.uk/entertainment/people/prince-harry-uncle-518512

Royston, Jack. "Princes' Divorce Agony: Prince Harry reveals his parents' marriage split left him and his brother William 'bouncing between two of them and never seeing either enough.'" *The Sun*, July 23, 2017. https://www.thesun.co.uk/news/4077245/prince-harry-has-revealed-the-effect-his-parents-divorce-had-on-him-and-william/

Samuelson, Kate. "A Detailed History of Prince Harry and Meghan Markle's Relationship." *Time*, November 27, 2017. http://time.com/5036452/prince-harry-meghan-markle-relationship-timeline/

# WORKS CONSULTED

Tweedie, Niel and Kallenback, Michael. "Prince Harry faces outcry at Nazi outfit." *The Telegraph*, January 14, 2005. http://www.telegraph.co.uk/news/uknews/1481148/Prince-Harry-faces-outcry-at-Nazi-outfit.html

# GLOSSARY

**courtship** (KOHRT-ship)–a period of dating that often precedes marriage

**diagnose** (dahy-uhg-NOHS)–to identify a medical condition through examination

**grief** (GREEF)–deep sorrow, especially after a death

**paparazzi** (POP-uh-rah-zee)–independent photographers who take pictures of celebrities

**polo** (POH-loh)–a game played on horseback with mallets and a wooden ball

**stigma** (STIG-muh)–a mark of shame

**swastika** (SWOS-ti-kuh)–a symbol of the Nazi Party

**tabloid** (TAB-loid)–a newspaper known for printing scandalous news, particularly about famous people

**vulnerable** (VUHL-ner-uh-buhl)–susceptible to being hurt

PHOTO CREDITS: Cover, pp. 1, 3, 4, 25, 26–Chris Jackson/Staff/Getty Images; p. 7–Jack Taylor/Stringer/Getty Images; p. 8–Karwai Tang/Contributor/Getty Images; pp. 11, 15, 16, 19, 21–PA Images/Alamy Stock Photo; p. 12–Patrick Riviere/Staff/Getty Images; p. 20–WENN US/Alamy Stock Photo; pp. 23, 27–WPA Pool/Pool/Getty Images. Artwork: Freepiks.

# INDEX